Who Has Spots?

Written by Lynn Anderson

Illustrated by Lily Toy Hong

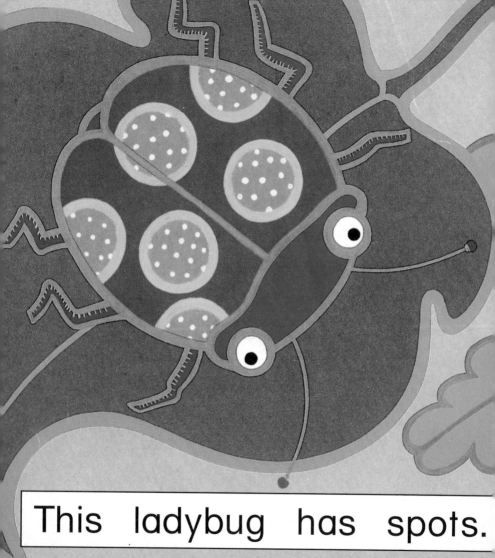

This ladybug has spots.

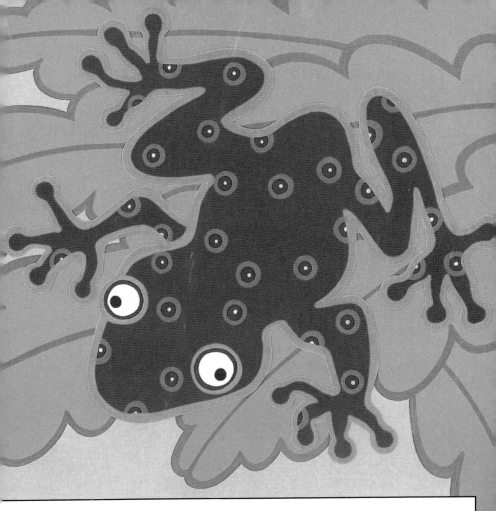

This frog has spots.

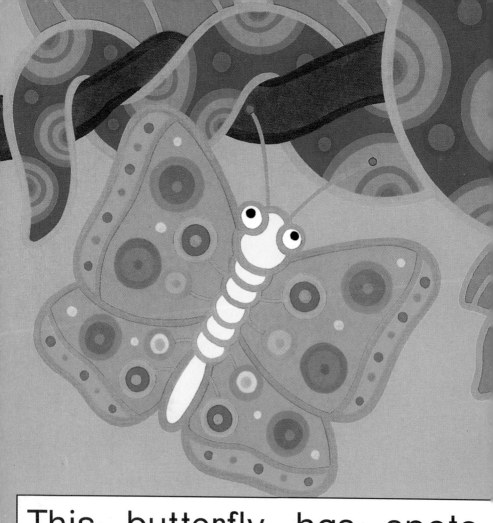

This butterfly has spots.

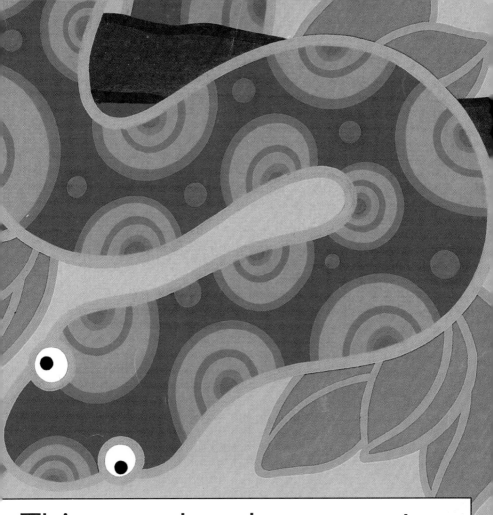

This snake has spots.

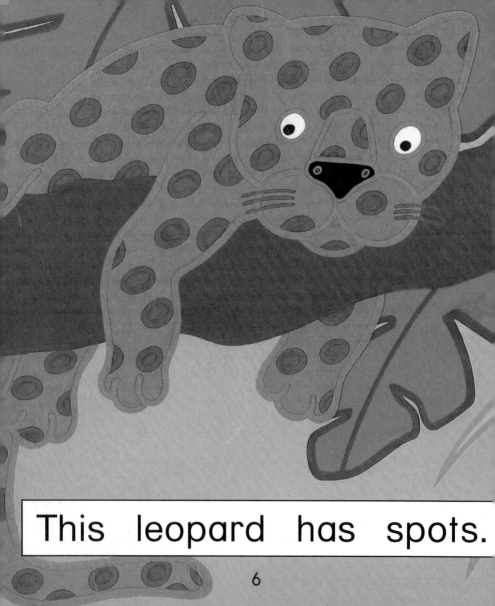

This leopard has spots.

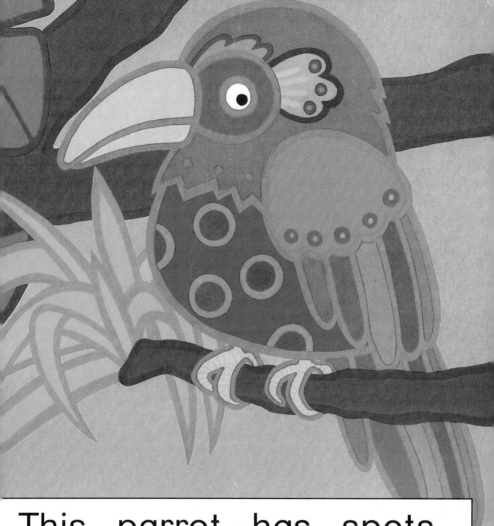

This parrot has spots.

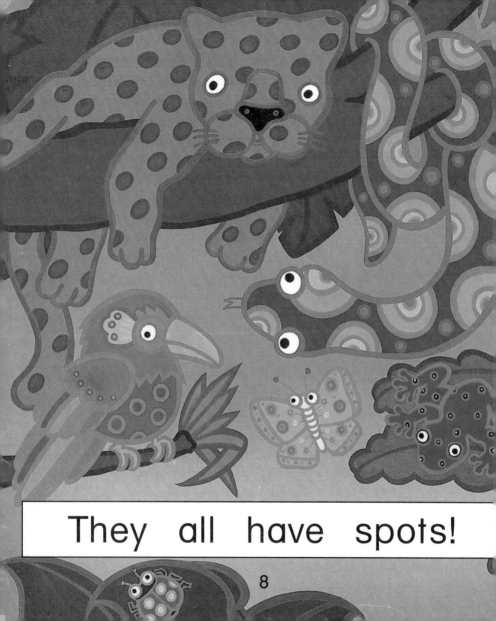

They all have spots!